PENDRAGON'S OBESSION

CORNELIA AMIRI

ABOUT PENDRAGON'S OBESSION

If the lover you craved night and day was forbidden to you… how far would you go to have them?

Eigyr is the woman for King Uthyr. A fiery dragon comet, sent by the gods, foretold she would bear his children.

There's one problem… she's married.

The brazen, powerful king awakens Eigyr's passion, but she will not forsake her wedding vows.

Driven by a burning desire, Uthyr will give anything to have but one night with Eigyr.

The druid, Menw, holds the power to fulfill the king's scandalous desire. With magic. But at what price?

GLOSSARY

In honor of this truly Welsh tale, I'm using the authentic Welsh names and spellings for the characters.

Arthyr (ar thur) – Legendary Welsh King and hero. It's usually written as Arthur.

Menw - (Meh nue} In the Welsh version of the King Arthyr tales there is a wizard who worked magic for Uthyr Pendragon. He was an enchanted knight of Arthyr's court as well. We've come to call him Merlin but I've kept his original name in this work.

Uthyr − (Ee ther) King Arthyr's father. It's usually seen written as Uther.

Gwrlais – (Gore lice) Duke of Cornwall and Eigyr's husband. It's usually written as Gorlois.

Eigyr − (AY-gir) The mother of King Arthyr. It's usually written as Igraine.

ONE

The gentle breeze blowing in off the Thames and the soft sun made for a pleasant Easter. Newly crowned King of the Britons, Uthyr, took his place at the banquet table. He didn't eat any of the dishes on the feasting board, for a woman had captured his gaze. Every dimple and curve of her luminous face called to him. Her radiant auburn hair and deep blue eyes, like the ones on a peacock's tail feathers, set his mind awhirl. He inhaled her fragrance, a swirl of lavender edged with musky hawthorn. His favorite smell had always been that of roasted meat, but he knew from now on it would be lavender and hawthorn...her scent.

She'd come with Gwrlais, her husband. They'd ridden to London at Uthyr's command, as had all the nobles in Britannia and their wives, daughter and sons. He'd summoned them to attend his coronation today.

Uthyr tore his gaze away from the most beautiful woman in all of Britannia to the duke sitting on the other side of her. "Did you and your lady wife," he nodded at the beauty, "have an enjoyable ride from Cornwall?"

"Most pleasant, my king." Gwrlais lifted his goblet and took a sip of mead.

Uthyr fixed his eyes back on the duke's wife. "And you, Lady Eigyr, is the feast to your liking?"

"It is grand, the food, the palace, your coronation."

Uthyr's gaze was captured by her temptingly plump lips the whole time she spoke to him. He licked his lips. "The palace was built for a Roman governor almost four hundred years ago. It's mine now...a Celtic palace."

Gwrlais set his goblet on the table with a clunk. "My king, we are Roman in part. Do we not take the best of both worlds?"

Uthyr jerked his head toward the duke. His jaw and neck tightened. "You sit at the board of a Celtic king. You are here to celebrate victories in the north and the imprisonment of Saxon warlords, Octa and Eosa, in this very city. Who brought that about?"

"Why, you brought us victories and captured those villainous Saxon leaders, my king."

"Yes, I and other Celts. Rome deserted us. I share no love of the long gone Romans. Nor should you as my duke."

Gwrlais bowed his head. "I misspoke, my king."

"Am I not called the Pendragon?"

"Indeed you are." The duke nodded in agreement.

"Is that not a Celtic title for leader?" Uthyr leaned back in his chair and glared at Gwrlais. The man had interrupted his conversation with Eigyr. "Pendragon, head-dragon, chief of the warriors ... King. So they say." He cut off a slice of pork on his plate and popped it into his mouth.

"It is so." Gwrlais tilted his chin up.

Uthyr ignored him. He felt woozy, almost mindless as he gazed into Eigyr's sparkling eyes. "The comet is the cause of it all. A blaze, hurtling through the sky, shaped into a fiery dragon with two serpentine tails. One lashed out beyond the old Celtic land of Gaul, the other reached towards the Irish Sea and unraveled into seven sparkling threads." He winked at Eigyr. "Menw, son of Teirwaedd, prophesied the fierce dragon tail that blazed beyond Gaul heralded a son, a king to hold power over all the kingdoms beneath his reach. Its other exhilarant tail symbolized a daughter, whose sons and grandsons would rule over Logres."

Eigyr laid her hand on the table by her plate. Uthyr covered her hand with his. "This morning I was crowned king, just as that comet foretold. Today I ordered my gold-smith to cast two mystical dragons of pure gold, one for each ray, my future heirs." The king gave her soft hand a squeeze. "Would you like me to have my goldsmith fashion a memento of this day for you? Perhaps a dragonhead brooch?"

The annoying duke cleared his throat loudly and Uthyr tilted his head toward him. "It is a tradition of Celtic hospitality for a chief to give gifts to his guests. Is it not?"

"You are generous, my king, but my wife has no need of a gold token to remember your coronation." Gwrlais spoke calmly but there was a hint of anger in his eyes.

"No, I do not, my king." Eigyr swallowed hard, clearly affected by the tension between her husband and her king. "I shall never forget this day." She spoke with sincerity.

"Nor I." Uthyr eased his hand off of hers but held her eyes with his gaze. Eigyr smiled at him with her mouth and her eyes.

Despite Menw's prophecy of children, Uthyr hadn't given any thought to settling down to a wife. Until now. He smiled back at Eigyr. The draw he felt toward this woman, the feeling she was his, overwhelmed him. Uthyr didn't think for one moment that Eigyr wouldn't prefer him to her husband. He'd been favored all his life. He was always the tallest, the fastest, the most handsome. Everyone loved Uthyr as a boy, and when he'd grown into a man ... he expected that same favoritism. And he always got it.

He tore his gaze away from Eigyr to look around the banquet hall, seeking his druid. Once his eyes fell on Menw, the statuesque, regal druid nodded at Uthyr.

Within his mind, Uthyr heard a smooth, calming voice that rang with wisdom. Without opening his mouth, Menw said to him alone, "She is the one. The Pendragon's mate. God Dewy, shapeshifter of the dragon, deems it so."

Menw knew all. Uthyr did not doubt him. But a moment of confusion flitted through his mind. *Eigyr is married to one of my nobles.* He popped a hot cockle in his mouth and chewed slowly as he gazed at Eigyr. *Does that matter... if the gods chose her as the mother of my children... the woman who will birth the mighty hero king of Britain and beyond?*

His hunger grew for more than food. How he longed to touch that silky hair plaited into six braids. He envisioned freeing each braid and watching the wealth of hair spill loose and spread across his bed as she lay upon it, ready to give herself to him.

"Scrumptious," he rasped as he smiled at her. He wanted her. Needed her. The gods wanted him to have her.

Eigyr returned his smile and he knew she wanted him, too. Uthyr's moment of doubt in pursing Gwrlais' wife vanished. Gwrlais no longer mattered to him.

"Yes, the cockles look delicious." Eigyr lifted the goblet to her lips and took a sip.

He meant her, not the shucked, steamed shellfish, but now he could offer her some since she seemed to like them.

"I am served the choice bits of all." He scooped up a small pile of cockles with his spoon and deposited them on her plate. If only he could feed them to her. Touch her luscious lips, watch them part, and push a cockle into her mouth. But her husband sat at her side and would no doubt make more foolish comments at such a gesture.

Of course, Uthyr was king. And a better man for her. Should not the most beautiful woman in the kingdom be with the most powerful man? She deserved nothing less than a true hero. Eigyr should be with the champion of Britannia...him...the Pendragon.

Her blue eyes gleamed with surprise as he shared the shellfish from his plate. Eigyr picked up a cockle with her slender fingers. She pressed it to her full lips, which formed a perfect circle. A surge of heat shot through him. He stiffened as she sucked the soft flesh deep into her mouth.

"Delicious." She licked her lips.

Uthyr's mouth watered with desire for this scrumptious woman. "Delightful." Still, he could not say the things he wanted to, here at the feasting table with her husband by her side. He had to keep his desire secret from Gwrlais. Otherwise he might try to stop Eigyr from coming to Uthyr. If he did, Uthyr would kill him.

As Eigyr devoured the cockles with relish, Uthyr shifted his gaze to his trusted friend, Ulfin, who sat further down at the table. Uthyr gestured to him and soon Ulfin stood at his side.

Ulfin leaned his head down and Uthyr whispered to him, "Have the cupbearer bring Eigyr a goblet with a note. It shall say she is more comely than any woman in Britain. And I beg to have a private word with her in my chambers after the feast. Sign it, Pendragon. Eigyr will withdraw the note, then the cupbearer will brim the goblet with mead." Uthyr fluttered his fingers in dismissal.

Ulfin headed toward the cupbearer to see to the task.

Uthyr grabbed his dagger and cut off a generous hunk of meat from the champion joint of wild boar. He inhaled the thick, savory scent as he stabbed the slab of pork with the point of his dagger and held it above Eigyr's plate. "The best portion for you, my lady."

"So generous, my king." Using her dagger, she pulled the slice of roasted boar onto her silver plate.

"I killed the beast myself in a boar hunt yesterday."

"You are a great hunter among your other many talents." Eigyr cut off a tiny piece.

"I love the hunt." Uthyr nodded. "I always capture what I seek." He flashed his most arresting smile. "Nothing gets away from me." He chuckled as he thought of how true that statement was, even going back to his childhood when, as a small boy, he'd chased squirrels through the woods.

"You should visit Cornwall, and we shall hunt for boar and stag." Gwrlais sliced the slab of roasted venison on his plate.

"I had other game and other games in mind." Uthyr raised an eyebrow as his gaze lingered on Eigyr.

"Whatever wild hunt you had in mind, I'm sure we can accommodate your taste in Cornwall." Eigyr's eyes brightened with an eager look.

"Yes, we have all sorts of game in Cornwall," Gwrlais said dryly.

Uthyr ran the sharp edge of his dagger across a slab of venison dripping with juniper berry sauce on his plate "I am sure you do." He tilted his head toward the lady he desired, knowing his longing for her burned in his eyes. "I have no doubt that in Cornwall, you truly possess what I seek most."

The cupbearer set a goblet in front of Eigyr. She picked it up, discreetly pulling out the strip of parchment so her husband did not see it. She brought it to her lap and glanced down, reading the note. Fluttering her long lashes, she looked up and met the king's gaze.

The cupbearer brimmed the goblet with mead from the jug he held.

Uthyr saw the movement of Eigyr's shoulder and realized she'd used that distraction to crumple the note and toss it on the floor.

"Let us enjoy the feast. Who can say what will happen after?" She flashed Uthyr a coy smile.

"It is fitting to plan a hunt while we enjoy this Easter feast." Gwrlais bit into it a piece of boar meat, chewing slowly, savoring it fully.

"I feel I am already on the hunt." Uthyr let out a deep, rich chuckle.

"Some prey should not be hunted." The duke swallowed his food. "What is this prey you speak of, my king?"

Eigyr glanced at her husband and her face clouded with uneasiness.

"As your king, I have no need to tell you what I wish to hunt." His voice was sharp and he glared daggers at Gwrlais. "Is this not true?"

They were Celts now, with no need to follow Roman ways. Celtic women could leave their husbands or take a lover any time they chose to. The decision was Eigyr's, not Gwrlais'. If she wanted to lie with her king, if she wanted to be his queen, so be it.

Uthyr looked out at all the nobles and their families supping at his board. "I dare say we have all had our fill ... of food. Let us all move into the palace gardens. Menw will strum his harp as we dance and make merry." He stood and called out in a voluminous tone, "Druid."

Menw tapped his feet rhythmically on the mosaic floor as he danced out of the banquet hall, strumming a harp in his arms. All the feasters rose from the long benches and followed him to the center courtyard.

So many left the room at once, all now with their backs turned to Uthyr, that he lost Eigyr in the crowd. No matter, he would find her in the other room and as everyone danced, he would sneak her away from prying eyes and ears, including those of the Duke of Cornwall.

As he stepped onto the lush green grass that carpeted the courtyard, he scanned the huge garden, searching for Eigyr. He stopped as he noticed that all eyes were upon him, for Menw was singing a paean to him.

The druid brushed his long, slender fingers across the strings of his harp.

With Pendragon at the helm,
The brave British Celts,
Crushed the seadogs.
Brave British Celts.

THEIR VICTORY WON.
The brave British Celts
Had the Saxons on the run.
Brave British Celts

HIDING *in peat bogs*
From the brave British Celts
And Pendragon

King of the brave British realm.
The brave British realm.

UTHYR LOVED music and had often been told he had a beautiful voice. But Uthyr was no bard. He was king. "My thanks for the best of songs." He nodded to Menw as the crowd of nobles and their families cheered. He took one step toward the druid, and at that moment two men rushed into the garden and ran to Uthyr.

Uthyr wheeled toward them. From years of warrior training, he grasped the hilt of the sword belted at his side. "Samson, Dubricius, what means this?"

"We tried to stop them." Samson's expression was like that of someone who'd been smacked in the face.

"We told him he could not go without your leave. As we are all here at your command," Duricius said with a grim scowl.

Uthyr set one hand on his hip. "Who left?" Even before he asked the question, he knew. He felt a gut-wrenching loss. The sensation was like having the breath knocked out of him, but worse. He'd felt fire and water, both passion and serenity, with Eigyr at his side during the feast. Now he felt empty.

"Gwrlais, Duke of Cornwall." Samson pointed in the direction of the old Roman road outside the palace.

"He rode off with his wife." Dubricius nodded. "Said he wouldn't lose what was dearest to him."

Uthyr stood there, trying to breathe. His neck and shoulders were wound so tight with tension, he had to fight the sensation that bent his head to a downcast position. He tilted his chin, holding his head high as he peered into Samson's eyes. "He took Eigyr." He clenched his fist and the emptiness was soon filled with boiling hot anger. Through clinched teeth, he ordered Samson and Dubricius, "Ride at once. Try to overtake him on the road. If you cannot, then gallop all the way to Cornwall." He brandished his fist in the air. "Tell Gwrlais to return to court at once, by command of the king."

Samson and Dubricius rode off to do his bidding. Uthyr bade everyone else to dance and make merry on this Easter day. Then he stomped off to his chamber and slammed the door.

In her brief time with him, Eigyr had given him a sense of completeness he'd not known he was missing until today. Now he'd let Gwrlais take her away. He'd lost what he needed most. It threw him off the path of his destiny and would leave him lonely and wanting the rest of his days, for no woman could compare to her...not for him.

Uthyr snatched the crown off his head and threw it hard against the wall as he let loose an ear-blasting, body-shaking, pain-filled yell, "Eigyr."

TWO

Eigyr clasped her hands together while she stood, unseen, in a small chamber off the front room of the castle. It was about the size of the pantry her sister had locked her inside when she was a small child, and then hadn't let her out until the end of the day. Her mother had searched for her that day, but Eigyr never told her what happened. She didn't want all the shouting and arguing. She liked quiet. Her family was loud, all of them. Her two older siblings and her younger one had never been quiet. She was the shy one. They were all always robust and healthy. Earaches plagued her in her childhood.

Maybe because the rest of my family was so noisy, she thought.

All grown up and married, she now had her ear to the wall, and her eye plastered to the small peek hole. And with so much practice at staying quiet, without making a sound, she secretly listened to the exchange between her husband and the king's man, Ulfin.

Gwrlais's champion, Jordan, stood at his side. She

should be at his side, not Jordan, but Gwrlais had dismissed her, saying this was man's talk. So Roman in his ways, Gwrlais saw a wife as more of a possession than a partner. He wasn't one to listen to any woman, and she needed someone to listen to her. Her family hadn't. She wished she had a husband who would. Especially now, as the tightness in her chest from worry had grown to the point of pain.

"I bring tidings from the king." Ulfin tilted his chin up and stood before the men in a warrior stance. "You left court without your sovereign's leave and disobeyed a royal summons to return. Settle your double affront to King Uthyr, or he will war against you and ravage your holdings."

No, please no, Eigyr thought. *He will never put aside his pride to apologize to the king. Gwrlais won't let any man take his wife. That is the way he sees it.*

Gwrlais stood before Ulfin, staring him down. "I merely protected what is mine, that most precious to me."

She stood silently behind the wall, wanting to scream at everyone. *Surely, Uthyr knows no good will come of this. The king could let this go. If he wants me, Uthyr must let me come to him on my own.*

"The king sees it differently. Return with me now. I cannot guarantee your life will be spared, but you may save your people." Ulfin's brows slanted downward. "If I return alone," he paused and swallowed hard, "there is no going back for you."

Eigyr shook with frustration, fear, and anger. *Foolish men. Gwrlais knows Uthyr will kill him, but what he fears is to let his woman go to another. That he sees as wrong. That he will not stand for.*

Gwrlais thrust his chest out. "My wife stays in Cornwall and I with her. Deliver that message to your king."

Eigyr held her arms over her chest. She knew if she didn't find some way to make this right, her people would die fighting with Gwrlais against the king. If such a battle ensued, she would be kept hidden behind a wall the whole time, just like now. Walled off from any say in the matter or any way to stop it. Like she was a child. Eigyr was through with hiding.

"No." She dashed toward the men. "Do not do this."

Gwrlais turned toward her. "You were to keep to your chambers."

"You cannot say you go to war over me. This is not my fault, but I will stop it." She pivoted toward Ulfin. "Tell the king the woman he wants will not have this. It's over. Gwrlais is my husband."

"It has gone beyond that. Your husband refused his king. If the Pendragon is not obeyed, chaos shall reign within Britannia and our enemies will rush forth and take all. The king must demand satisfaction for your husband's insult."

The stress weighed on her. She felt like spiders crawled all over her body. "But it is not my fault." She clenched her fist. "Not my fault."

"Come." Gwrlais took her into his arms, comforting her.

"No." She pulled out of his arms. "You could die." She wheeled toward Ulfin. "The king could be killed. Stop this madness now."

"Surrender to me." Ulfin arched one eyebrow as he gazed hard at Gwrlais. "Spare the innocent."

"I fight for what is mine." Gwrlais set his hand on Eigyr's shoulder in a possessive gesture and pulled her behind him as if to shield her. "I will meet the Pendragon on the battlefield."

Ulfin nodded. With sadness in his eyes, he slowly turned and left the castle.

Eigyr grabbed her husband's forearms. "What will you do now?"

"In truth, the king's army outnumbers mine. So much so, I cannot meet him in the field. I must garrison the castles until I can get help. More men."

"You mean to turn to our enemies: Saxons, Scotts, the Irish that invade us?" Eigyr released her husband and clasped her hands to her face.

"If I have to."

"You are mad. You are all mad, and the king too." Eigyr rubbed her forehead hard, turned her back to her husband and Jordan. She ran out of the entranceway and up the stairs to her chamber and threw herself onto her bed. With her face sunk into the pallet, she released her pain and her fury in a torrent of tears and wailing. She didn't care who heard her.

Her shuddering stopped and she caught her breath. As she lay on the plaid bedspread, moist with her tears, she saw Uthyr in her mind as clearly as when she'd sat at his side at the feasting board. His dark brown hair highlighted with sparse strands of copper, the set of his eyes, nose, and mouth on his oval face, all proportioned with the perfection of a master sculptor's hand. He was a living piece of art, more beautiful than any of the busts that had decorated the temples and government buildings before the Roman army left. Unlike those statues, Uthyr seemed indestructible. Even though he was only flesh and blood, one could easily believe the ancient dragon god Dewy championed him, for no one could best him in battle. With Uthyr against him, Gwrlais was as good as dead. She couldn't do anything to stop it.

If only she had never wed Gwrlais. She had only agreed to the betrothal because it had given her an opportunity to finally please her father and mother. But they probably just wanted to get rid of her: the quiet, sickly family outcast. They never came to visit. None of them.

But Uthyr, he was the kind of man she would marry to please herself. There was something she did to please herself that Gwrlais knew nothing about. She often imagined herself an ancient Celt, dancing around a bonfire on Beltane. She'd strip off every piece of her clothing and dance nude in broad daylight in her bower...with the door open. Her ladies, her servants knew, but no one else.

The moment any man stepped down the hall, including Gwrlais, she would dash naked to the door, shut it, then throw her clothes on as fast as she could. She loved the dancing, the freedom, and she loved the danger of almost getting caught, of someone finding out that instead of a reserved, dutiful wife, she was a mad vixen.

When she danced around this imagined bonfire, Uthyr was the man she imagined herself dancing with. She thought he came from her imagination. Then she met him at his Easter coronation. He was real and he wanted her. He would wage a war to win her. How terrible and wonderful at the same time. She lifted her head from the bed and wiped her eyes with her hands.

THE KING SLAMMED his fist down hard on the small, oak-hewn table. "Eigyr should be mine." A gleaming, solid gold dragon quivered on the table with the vibrations of his rage. Ale sloshed from the clay jug beside it. "Not Gwrlais'."

He could feel the warmth of her body against him as if

he held Eigyr. Her lavender scent danced in his nostrils as if she was with him. His need for the woman was so strong that if she was not with him in flesh and blood, he envisioned that she was.

Uthyr peered through the open flap of his tent at his vast siege army. Instead of having Eigyr to look at, he had this. Soldiers drilling, clanging their metal swords together as they blocked each other's blows. Shaggy war dogs barked in the background as many of his men huddled about small fires, drinking and gambling, biding time for the siege to break.

Instead of Eigyr he had a siege. When Gwrlais retreated to Dimilioc, Uthyr led his army here and blocked all roads to and from the stronghold. Yet he was no closer to holding Eigyr in his arms. The woman wasn't even at Dimilioc. Uthyr nodded as Ulfin entered the tent.

His friend's clear, blue eyes were wide with concern. "My king, what course do we take now?"

He grabbed the clay jug beside the steadfast dragon and filled his goblet with ale. "I can think of nothing but Eigyr." Uthyr drew the cup to his lips and then froze. "I must win her or die of longing for the woman."

"She is at Tintagel." Lines at Ulfin's brows and eyes deepened. "Perched on a mountain top at the edge of the churning sea, the fortress is unbreachable. There is only one entrance, so narrow it would take no more than three of Gwrlais' men to defend the gateway against an entire army."

Heaviness built up in Uthyr's chest. He drank the ale in one long gulp as he watched something flicker in his friend's lucid, blue eyes.

Ulfin paused and took a deep breath. "You might obtain Eigyr ... with druid magic." He rubbed his lips together.

"Magic." Uthyr set the empty goblet down with a clunk. "The druid claims Eigyr is my destiny. It has to do with that comet and the dragon god Dewy." He rested his hand on the gold dragon's scaly back. "Bring Menw to me."

THREE

Ulfin returned to the Pendragon's tent and announced, "My king, the wise man, Menw."

The druid sported a thick mustache on an otherwise beardless face. His long brown hair fell past his shoulders in the old Celtic way. Menw strode to Uthyr, who sat on a Roman cot as if it was his throne.

Uthyr nodded at Menw. Though masculine and well balanced, the druid's features transformed with his moods. When his inner self was as still water, his features were soft. When he was a whirling storm, his features were sharp. Uthyr had even heard that Menw's eyes changed color from brown, to blue, green, even amber. The energy surging within him was so intense, his emotions affected anyone near. One human body could not contain them.

"My king, how may I be of service?" Menw's tone and expression were serene.

Uthyr felt hopeful by just being around the druid. "My deepest desire goes unfulfilled. I burn for Eigyr. Day and night, I hear the silky purr of her voice in my head and ripples of heat course through me. I cannot think, I can barely breathe. I do not possess the patience of druids. Long before I was king, from childhood onward, I have grown accustomed to getting anything I ask for. I've been told it's my smile that does it." He flashed his most devastating grin at Menw. "I must have her now." He held his breath, waiting for the druid to help him.

Menw's expression grew soft as if he knew the suffering Uthyr was going through. If the legends held true, the sage could read the minds of men as easily as others listened to spoken words. "To gain a tryst with Eigyr, you must make use of magical arts not heard of in your time. With the blessing of the old gods, I can transform you into the exact image of the Duke of Cornwall. You will appear as none other than Gwrlais."

He met Menw's gaze. "How can this be?"

"In the sacred grove you will metamorphose into Gwrlais, and Ulfin into the semblance of Jordan. While I, in the appearance of his other friend, will make the third in the adventure." Menw leaned forward. "With our flawless disguises, we will be welcomed into the fortress of Tintagel."

He clasped Menw's shoulder. "My greatest thanks."

Uthyr turned to Ulfin. "Inform the commanders, I leave them in charge of the siege." Whether Uthyr lay with Eigyr or not, Gwrlais still had to be dealt with. Uthyr knew a man who would dare to disobey his king was most likely capable of killing his king. His two brothers, King Constans and King Aurelius Ambrosius, and his father, King Constantine, were slain by their enemies. Gwrlais was his enemy. But now his mind was filled only with thoughts of Eigyr. He would leave Gwrlais' fate in the hands of his commanders, for now. "I am on a mission of stealth, say naught more."

"As you wish, my king." Ulfin bowed his head.

ULFIN MET up at the horse pen with Uthyr and Menw, who had already saddled the horses. The adventurous trio vaulted onto the steeds and rode swiftly toward the sacred copse. The moon rose over the wild temple of ancient trees, where they dismounted. Menw led them into a circle of nine yews with scaly bark and dark foliage.

A silver cauldron, hallowed with images of the gods, stood there. Round, luminescent and magical like the newly risen moon.

Menw drew back his plaid cloak, revealing leather pouches of herbs tied at his waist. He turned to the king's friend. "Gather fallen branches and twigs."

Ulfin went to his task while Uthyr picked up the silver cauldron. He carried it beyond the yew trees, leaving Menw within the shadows of the dark grove.

Halting at a small stream, he filled the vessel with pure, fresh water. Uthyr returned to the copse and set the sacred cauldron on the stack of wood Ulfin had gathered.

Menw raised his arms high in the air and drew the heat, pulsating through his body, down to his fingers. He conjured a spark of fire out of his hand. With a flick of his wrist, the spark caught and spread through the kindling.

Uthyr gasped, too astonished to speak.

The wizard invoked the fire, "Glowing amber power, move through all things, seen and unseen."

A trickle of smoke surrounded the silver cauldron and rose in the air. The evening darkness faded, aglow from the robust blaze. From a worn, brown leather pouch, Menw withdrew a handful of garlic. He tossed the smelly cloves into the fire, which flared into a bright burst. He sank to his knees, his elbows and chest touched the ground, connected to the earth. Gazing into the amber fire, he chanted to the flames.

"Images burn away.
Metamorphose at hand.
For love's sake,
without delay,
I bid remake
king of the land,
liken to the husband.
Hearts and bodies as one,
thus conceive a son,
of valor and sincerity,
famous to posterity.
So mote it be."

At his words, the flames rushed upwards. "Envision your transformation." Menw reached toward Uthyr, palm up with his fingers curled. "In your mind's eye, become Gwrlais. Take on each feature of his physical image."

The druid turned his dark, piercing gaze onto Ulfin. "Imagine you are his friend, Jordan, in every way, with no trace of your true self."

Uthyr did as the druid ordered. He stood there, imagining he looked just like the Duke of Cornwall. He clasped his hands together. Soon, Eigyr would be his. Along with Menw and Ulfin, he waited for the water in the silver cauldron to bubble like the foam on the waves at sea.

Menw drew his hand into a soft pouch and pulled out nine plump hawthorn berries. The druid crushed them in his fingers and dropped the crushed red berries into the roaring water. He called upon the god of the sea, "Manawydan fab Llyr, I invoke your power.

"God of transformation,
tricks and illusion.
with magical infusion
of druid application,
Metamorphose at hand.
For love's sake,
I bid remake
king of the land
liken to the husband.
Hearts and bodies as one,
thus conceive a son
of valor and sincerity,
famous to posterity.
So mote it be."

White steam rose from the cauldron. Sweat beaded Uthyr's brow from the heat of the flames. Menw reached into a crinkled leather pouch and tossed a pinch of frankincense into the silver pot. Its essence perfumed the air. From another pouch, he drew out and threw in a dollop of reddish-brown myrrh. The sharp, somewhat bitter scent rose in the air. From a third pouch, he grabbed a pinch of vervain and scattered it over the bubbling water.

Menw swept his arm over the boiling brew. The water and herbs flowed in that direction as he magically stirred it nine times. Unfastening a gold goblet from his belt, he scooped up a cupful of potion. He handed it to the king.

Uthyr paused a moment to muster his courage. It was too late to turn back now if he wanted to. Menw had cast his magic and soon it would take hold. He blew on the steamy brew to cool it. Then he took a few sips of the hot, bittersweet concoction. He passed the cup to Ulfin, who took a gulp and handed the last portion to Menw, who drank his fill. The triad of king, friend, and wizard shut their eyes as the shape shifting began.

With a prickling sensation in his fingers and toes, Uthyr's body changed into the image of Duke Gwrlais, his foe and rival. He ran his hands over his face. Uthyr felt his nose grow longer, his cheeks flatten, and his skin sag. He'd done it, turned himself into Gwrlais to have Eigyr. Anything for Eigyr.

When Uthyr shifted his gaze, he felt funny. Then, he realized his eyes were narrower, now shaped like Gwrlais', and things looked a little different. He peered at his friend. Instead of a golden tan with olive undertones, Ulfin's complexion was pale with pink tones and he was taller and broader.   "Ulfin is that you? You look just like Jordan." Uthyr trembled when he heard his own voice. "I sound like an old man."

"Ulfin is that you?" Uthyr trembled when he heard his own voice. "I sound like an old man."

"My king, not only is your voice that of the duke's, but you are the image of him in every feature." Ulfin let out a wry chuckle. "I cannot believe my eyes."

"Menw, is it you?" Uthyr chortled. "I swear you're Bricel. Your hair is short like a Roman's."

Menw flashed a mischievous smile. "You have a bald spot in the middle of your head, Duke Gwrlais."

Still laughing, Uthyr clapped the druid on the back. "You've done it." He felt his throat tighten as he realized he would finally be alone with the woman he craved, he needed, that he somehow...loved. "You've given me what no one else could. Eigyr." He placed his hand on his chest as he peered at the man who now looked like Bricel. "What can I do to repay you?"

Even in the form of Bricel, Menw's gaze was intense as he stared at Uthyr. "I shall tell you when the time comes."

Uthyr nodded at Menw wondering what the druid would ask for. Then he vaulted onto his horse. Menw eased onto his mount and Ulfin climbed into his saddle. The journey to Tintagel began.

FOUR

The air tingled with the magic of twilight as the triad neared the fortress, cast in black against the fading light.

Ulfin, at the lead, goaded his horse up steep steps cut into the rock, leading to a mountain stronghold perched above a tumultuous sea. Ulfin and Menw followed him on their mounts.

Shadows danced in the mountains, enchantment hung in the moonlit sky. Salty, damp air rose from the foamy water below. Seagulls screeching lonely cries into the strong wind soared above the trio, who forced their horses onward. Their steeds' hooves clung to the rough path.

Uthyr came to the end of the treacherous path. His heart stilled as he waited for the gatekeeper. He let out a long sigh when the gate opened. The smiling porter, thinking he was Gwrlais, bid a warm welcome to him and his friends.

Uthyr's heart hammered. He could barely believe he'd be with her. At any moment, he'd actually hold Eigyr in his arms. Torches flickered against the rough stone wall of the hall as he headed to Eigyr's royal bower. Anticipation, like the racing of his heart, increased with every step.

He didn't know which room was hers, so in the tone and timbre of Gwrlais' voice, Uthyr yelled out, "I have come back to you."

"Gwrlais." The sound of Eigyr's melodic voice flowed down the hall.

Uthyr's heart beat erratically. He ran toward the most beautiful sound he'd ever heard. Since childhood, the chirp of a cricket and crow of a rooster were like music to him. But the love of those sounds had given way to his love of Eigyr's voice.

He halted before the wooden door to her chamber. Waves of excitement swept through him.

He knocked his knuckles against the thick oak door as he tried to catch his breath. She opened the door. It wasn't a dream. He stood there, face to face with Eigyr.

He drank in the visage of her dainty face and sparkling eyes, which drew him into their depths. She wore only a long white tunic. He swept his gaze across her breast, which heaved above a whittled waist and flat stomach. Her long legs were draped to the thighs by a cascade of long, glistening auburn hair, freed from its braids. Her lips drew into a pout and she tilted her head in puzzlement.

A ripple of fear shot through him as a voice inside asked, *Does she suspect me? Can she tell who I am?* A great warrior, the king of the land, the Pendragon, never lacked for bravery, but now he stood frightened by this woman. She might not return his affections. But tonight he was Gwrlais...the man she married.

"What happened? Why have you left Dimilioc?"

He barely heard what she asked, his concentration waning, intoxicated with desire for her. Eigyr's alluring scent danced in an invisible cloud around his head. Those lush lips, so near, within reach, taunted and teased him. His heart pounded harder. So close, he ached to touch her soft skin.

When he did not answer, she stepped back.

Fearing she might grow suspicious, he recalled the story he'd created to cover his sudden arrival. He cleared his throat. "Be not alarmed." He stepped inside her bower and closed the door behind him. "Though Dimilioc is under siege by the king, I left to ride through the night to protect Tintagel, for you are here."

"You risked falling into the hands of the Pendragon, just to come here to keep me safe." She wrapped her smooth arms around his neck. "I love you so."

A jolt of heat shot through him at the contact. His arms encircled her waist and he pulled her even closer, clasping her body against his. His throat tightened from the over-powering joy. He swallowed hard and in a ragged whisper he said, "I've longed for you so."

"And I you."

He felt the rise and fall of her breast against his chest as he crushed her to him.

Her breath was warm against his face as she said, "I can't help but think of Uthyr."

Flattered by her interest he smiled. "You think of Uthyr?"

"I fear he means to do his worse to you. I do not want to lose you over the Pendragon's jealousy."

His body tensed. "Am I not here with you now, while the king is far away in Dimilioc?" Uthyr fought his annoy-ance. After all, she thought he was her husband, that was why she called the king jealous and spoke of her concerns for Gwrlais. "This eve is not for fear. It is for pleasure. On this enchanted night, we have each other." With a gentle sway, he rocked her back and forth. As his body brushed against Eigyr, his skin burned.

"Yes, you are right," Eigyr said in a breathy voice. "I don't want to think of anything but you. I don't want to be anywhere but here in your arms."

He slid one hand to her dainty chin and cupped it with great tenderness. He tilted her lips to his. His mouth pressed against the warm, velvety texture of her lips. As he tasted her lips he inhaled her lavender scent. Tenderly, he rubbed his lips against hers, caressing them. He pressed his mouth harder against hers in a more demanding kiss. She let out a soft moan. His erection pressed hard against his braies. Desperately, he wanted to tear his pants off. He wanted to rip Eigyr's tunic off her even more. He wanted to touch, to feel the softness of every inch of her bare body.

He slid his hand beneath her tunic and brushed his palm against the smooth flesh of her thigh and hip. The pressure in his groin deepened. His erection grew heavier. His cock twitched. His mind was filled with the intensity of standing here with Eigyr. She sent all his senses reeling.

Uthyr prodded his tongue against her lips, parting them. He thrust his tongue inside her open mouth. He plunged his tongue in and out of her warm, moist mouth. Reluctantly, he eased his lips off hers to take a breath. His lips still burned from the kiss. He stepped back and stooped slightly grabbing the hem of her tunic with both hands. He yanked the garment off over her head.

She stood nude before him. He raked his gaze over her, drinking in the beauty of her round breasts, her curves, and the triangle nest of tiny red hairs at her crotch.

Her mouth twisted with amusement. "I wear naught, but you are still fully clothed."

His pulse raced. "As you wish, my lady." His cock swelled and strained beneath his braies. It felt different somehow. Strange. Then he recalled he was different. He had Gwrlais' body. He couldn't think about the differences too much, his need for Eigyr was so great. A burning desire coiled so tight in him, he couldn't wait to get his clothes off. He pulled at his chain mail to remove it.

"I cannot help you with your armor. Even you cannot remove it alone. It is too heavy." Eigyr's soft laughter filled the air. "You usually don't enter our chamber with armor."

"I was in a rush to see you." He grinned. "Wait right here." He darted out of the chamber and briskly walked up to Ulfin and Menw, who waited for him. "Help me with my chain mail and sword." They assisted him right away and laid both on the bench where they'd been seated.

"The servants keep looking at us because we're just sitting here. We need to go to our chambers," Ulfin said.

Menw whispered to Uthyr. "We don't know where they are."

He whispered back, "I am sure the wisest sage in the realm and my right hand man can figure out where their sleeping chambers are." He laughed. "I will not see either of you until morning. I will be with Eigyr...alone...the entire night." He turned and hurried back to Eigyr's bower.

"THAT'S BETTER," Eigyr said, standing totally bare by the bed.

He'd never seen a more beautiful sight in his life. He stepped up to her. She was his ... this night. Though she thought he was another man.

Uthyr gazed into her smoldering eyes. He touched her

dainty ear and ran his finger down the back of it and along her jawbone. *How could skin be so soft, so smooth?*

She took his hand and brought it to her mouth. Parting her plump lips and taking the finger he'd touched her with, she sucked it. His finger tingled as she sensuously slid it in and out of her mouth. He shut his eyes for a moment, moved by the sensations spiraling through him.

She withdrew her lips from his moist finger. His breath grew so shallow he was in a near pant. He tilted his head until he covered her hot, wet lips with his.

Eigyr fondled his curly locks. Her soft fingers in his hair caused a mellow sensation as if transporting him to a beach. Sea waves rushing in, wetting his feet as his toes sank deep into the shifting sand and the warm sun caressed him as a gentle breeze ruffled his hair.

Eigyr eased her lips off his. Uthyr's breath caught in his throat as she reached down, grabbed the hem on his tunic and raised it up over his head, then tossed it to the floor.

A bubble of joy rose in his throat. "Eigyr, my love."

She grabbed his belt and unfastened it. Hooking her fingers in the waistband of his braies, she slid them down his legs until she knelt before him. Picking up one foot at a time, he kicked the braies off his feet.

He helped her up, drew her into his arms and whirled her in the air, like a leaf lifted by the breeze. Cradling her in his arms, he carried her to the bed and as he laid her down, she let out a low, whispery moan.

He wished he could tell her who he was. She willingly gave herself to him because she thought he was Gwrlais. And what if a babe came from this night, the son that Menw foretold? To her he was the king...not her lover...not her husband. She willingly gave herself to him because she thought he was Gwrlais. And what if a babe came from this night, the son that Menw foretold? The prince, symbolized by the dragon comet. One who would hold power over kingdoms as far as Gaul. Could it be that his son would grow up thinking Gwrlais was his father?

Thick red tresses streamed down the curvy lines of her milky flesh. Past her jutting rose-tipped breast to her chiseled waist, and the cutest navel in the center of her flat stomach. Then all the way down to her rounded hips. As he gazed upon her, the tightness in his groin intensified, squeezing his balls and his cock. His mind focused only on her. Her wants, her needs. He cringed at his guilt for deceiving her.

He would tell his son and Eigyr the truth one day, when they could understand this was all the will of the gods. For it was the gods themselves who chose her as the mother of his children ... the woman destined to birth the mighty hero king of Britannia and beyond.

Placing one knee on the pallet, Uthyr crawled on the plaid spread slowly, like a lion to his prey, towards this woman, who lay there, awaiting him. Gwrlais's woman. But tonight the gods gave her to him.

Uthyr slipped his legs over hers. Eigyr's legs were so shapely, so smooth. Her warm, yielding body stretched out beneath his, taking his weight as he covered her.

The heat from her flesh spread through every fiber of his being. Fiercely, he smothered her lips with his. He twisted his mouth against her moist, willing lips. Blasts of heat surged through him. His tongue grazed the softness of her mouth and then slid between her parted lips. He swept his tongue around her mouth. Her velvet tongue tangled with his.

She stroked the sides of his body then grasped his thighs, digging into his flesh with her nails. Uthyr was grabbed by the overwhelming urge to thrust his cock into her soft, sex.

Eigyr skimmed her hands down his body and danced her fingers across the hardened, bulging flesh of his arousal, stroking back and forth.

Soon, he would burst in her hand. "May I gaze into your sweet core?" Uthyr barely recognized his own voice, so hoarse and throaty, he could barely speak. He blinked his eyes, overcome with the intensity of the moment. This was it? Would she say no? Would she yes, but only out of wifely duty to Gwrlais? He held his breath, waiting for her answer.

"Yes, my love." Spreading her long, creamy legs wide, she offered herself to him.

He ached with a fierce need as he peered into her tight, wet channel. Uthyr sank his finger into her. She panted and moaned as he churned her creamy pussy.

He withdrew his hand. She gasped and watched, mesmerized as he jabbed his finger between his lips and sucked. Licking every drop of her intoxicating elixir off his finger.

"Spread the folds of your pussy for me," he rasped as his heart beat wildly.

Eigyr slid her hand to the nest of tiny curls and stroked her finger into the wet folds. She let out a soft gasp followed by a breathy sigh. She spread her entrance open in full to him.

Uthyr dipped his head and flicked his tongue against her clit. Eigyr inhaled hard. Her body jerked. He whisked the hard nub with his tongue. She whimpered with plea-sure. He gazed at her pink pussy, wet with need. As he licked her slick slit up and down, he felt her fingers tremble. She withdrew her hand. Intoxicated by the salty, tangy taste of her, he delved his tongue inside her pussy. She drew in sharp breaths as he flicked his tongue within the moist heat of her channel. He stroked her, gliding his tongue in and out.

She drew in sharp breaths as he flicked his tongue within the heat of her channel. He lifted his head and took in the rapt expression on her face. With her eyes shut, she drew her lips into an open circle and her entire body trembled in ecstasy from the pleasure he'd given her.

As her breath slowed, she fluttered her long lashes, and with open eyes she peered at him. "Please ... come to me," Eigyr rasped. "I need you."

Uthyr straddled her hips. Wrapping his fingers around his hard erection, he brushed it up and down her slit. He took a deep breath and prodded her tight entrance with the head of his cock. He barely dipped the mushroom-shaped tip into her, then pulled out. He inched in and out, again and again, heightening the pleasure to come, driving her and him mad. He couldn't hold back a moment longer. He sank his cock into the depths of her tight pussy. Eigyr bucked with the impact of his thrusts.

"I love you so," Eigyr called out in a breathy voice.

"Not as much as I love you," he rasped. The gods help his soul, he was in love with her. She didn't even know who he was.

"We won't let the king come between us." Her tone sounded like she was questioning him. As if she waited for an answer from him. A confession.

Did she suspect? He swallowed hard. No, she couldn't possibly. He didn't recognize himself. She welcomed him into her body because she thought he was her husband, his enemy, his rival... Gwrlais. The man he envied most in the world. "No one will come between us," he answered.

His father King Constantine was slain by his enemies,

and his oldest brother King Constans. He and his brother, Aurelius, had come back to England to avenge them. Then Aurelius was crowned king and poisoned by his enemies. Now Uthyr, the last of his family, was king. He had to slay his enemies before they killed him. Gwrlais' days were numbered, but for now all Uthyr could think of was Gwrlais' wife.

A sensation of intense pleasure engulfed every pore of his body as he pumped into her, plunging deeper each time. As he pressed harder, her moans grew deeper, more desperate. The rhythm fired his blood even more. He plunged again and again into her pulsating pussy. Mad with lust, and love and Menw's enchantments, most of all, mad with want for Eigyr.

She arched her hips, meeting his thrust. She arched her hips, meeting his thrust. His breathing sounded like waves crashing against the shore.

His breathing sounded like waves crashing against the shore. The sensation of a rising, liquid fire consumed him. They quivered in release. Uthyr spilled his seed into her as he moaned, mindlessly. His body stilled and his pounding pulse slowed as his breath grew steadier. He would deal with Gwrlais for good. Eigyr was his. Wrapping his arms around her, Uthyr rolled over so she lay on top of him.

FIVE

Eigyr gazed at.Gwrlais. He was so attentive, so excited by her body. It flamed the need in her. Made her hot and bothered ... mad with desire. If he had brought her to such heights of plea-sure before, she wouldn't have noticed Uthyr. When he'd placed his mouth between her thighs, she'd come undone ...all sparks and fire bursting into an explosion. He'd never made love to her with his mouth before. Her thoughts set her heart racing, pounding hard in her chest.

He'd always treated her like a possession, a treasured, fragile jewel. Not like a woman he wanted to give his body and soul to, like he did tonight. He was a burning fire, all fervid and wild. The moment his lips covered hers, he released the hunger in her for fierce, unbridled sex with the man she dreamed of. The man she loved. A small voice in her head said, *my husband*. But she had doubts.

He even felt different inside her. Longer. Thicker. She had lain with Gwrlais many a night, but he'd never filled her with mindless pleasure that sang in her veins before.

It made no sense that this man was anyone other than

Gwrlais. He looked like and sounded like her husband. But he didn't act like him. His body didn't move the way Gwrlais had in bed. This Gwrlais had more grace, more zest, more strength, more passion.

He wasn't Gwrlais. No matter who this man looked like, he wasn't her husband. This lover could only be the king... the pendragon.

Still, she had said nothing to him. She hadn't asked him any questions that would prove or disprove his true identity. She had mentioned the king, but when he did not give himself away, she said nothing more of it. If she confirmed her suspicions she might feel a need to stop, to put an end to the encounter, and she didn't want to. She had longed to be taken into Uthyr's arms the moment he so brazening flirted with her at the coronation feast.

Now she'd show him how much she loved him. All the while she'd let him think she didn't know who he was. That's what he deserved for trying to fool her. This wasn't all Uthyr, though. This was magic, and the greatest druid in the land served the king.

Eigyr knew something was different about Gwrlais besides his sudden passion for her. It puzzled her since the moment he arrived. Now she realized it was the fragrance of his body. A man's sweat and body scent can't suddenly smell different. This was a different man.

She blinked her eyes to settle her thoughts. She set her free hand on his inner leg and stroked his muscular thigh. He looked identical to her husband. Though not a young man, Gwrlais had a warrior's body, but not as toned or as muscular as Uthyr's.

No man could compare to Uthyr. The king stood as tall and strong as a woodland tree. His lush, thick hair was always wild, never fully combed. A look of wildness suited

Uthyr. He always looked like he'd just come from a battle or the bed of one of the many women who gave themselves to him. But he had not waged war or transformed his appearance with druid magic for any of them.

One thing set her mind at ease: she at least knew he had not killed her husband. For he would not disguise himself as Gwrlais unless Gwrlais still lived. Her husband was safe for now. Because she lay with his greatest enemy.

She sat between his thighs and wrapped her fingers around his smooth, slick flesh. Flicking her wrist, she slid her hand from the base to the tip, reviving his cock to its full power and beauty. She lowered her head and licked his salty, tangy flesh from the bottom to the top. His cock twitched. She felt it swell and harden beneath her fingers. She swirled her tongue over the mushroom head.

She shut her eyes and imagined Uthyr's face as she'd kissed his cock. The image of the king ignited her passion more than her own husband's appearance. Uthyr was arresting. His flesh so toned and firm, his physique so beautiful, chiseled. Such manly features, his firm chin, piercing blue eyes and his height, so statuesque. He exuded heat and energy. Uthyr wanted to kill her husband. Yet she knew ... she lay with him now. What a bad wife she was.

But no one would ever know. Her thoughts, her feelings were her secret. She looked up and peered at the body of her husband as he lay nude on the bed, bathed in candle-light. She peered into his eyes. She gazed not into Gwrlais' soul but Uthyr's. Even he didn't realize that she knew who he actually was.

She shifted her gaze to his crotch. Opening her mouth, she stretched her lips over the head of his cock. She slid her hand from his aroused flesh to his balls and rolled one then the other in the palm of her hand. She leaned down, smothering his hardening flesh in full. His long cock pressed against the back of her throat. Her mouth eased and relaxed around the fullness of his flesh. She had an acute ache, a fiery yearning in her pussy. She glided her mouth upwards then down again. As she slid his cock in and out of her mouth, he released a fierce moan. She inhaled the seductive musky scent of his arousal.

She squeezed her lips tighter around his aroused flesh. Her heart raced as she skimmed her fingertips over his balls in feathery strokes. His heaving breath sounded fast and hard. Her own breathing grew shallow. He let out long, deep moans. She drew her lips off him as his entire body quivered in a spasm. She let out a breathy sigh as she gazed at Gwrlais' face.

He let out long, deep moans as his entire body quivered in a spasm. His semen spewed into her mouth and she drew her lips off him.

She let out a breathy sigh as she gazed at Gwrlais' face. His eyes were half closed from rapt pleasure. A wide open smile spread across his face. She straddled his muscular thighs, positioning her pussy over his bulging flesh. With her hand, she guided him inside. A hot shiver spread through her body as she sank down on him. Their bodies joined, she gazed into his eyes now open, sparkling with desire.

Groaning, he arched his cock deeper into her. Lifting her hips, she began the age-old rhythm of love play. Their bodies rocked back and forth. She felt the swish of her hair across her back, shoulders and face as she rode him hard. She shut her eyes as a flaming sensation flowed through her. She inhaled the scent of the burning wax from the lighted candles. She opened her eyes and saw him reaching for her jiggling breasts.

He cupped one in each hand and kneaded her aching breasts. She sucked the air in through her teeth as the sensation intensified the pleasure spiraling through her. His breathing grew harsh and uneven as he squeezed her tingling breasts. She bounced upon him as he bucked beneath her.

Her nipples hardened beneath his warm palms. He released her breasts and slid his fingers to her erect peaks. He flicked both nipples with his fingers. She clenched his erection with her pussy, squeezing hard. He rolled the tips with his thumbs. She ground his powerful flesh. He pinched her nipples. A cry of delight broke from her lips.

Eigyr burned with need as she glided up and down his cock, quickening the pace. Breathless panting turned to rapt shrieks. Her pussy clamped down hard on his cock.

He called out her name in a deep, throaty voice. "Eigyr."

Her body shook in a spasm of release as his hot semen flowed into her. Eigyr's breath slowed to a steady pace and her quivering stopped. She gazed at his body, which glistened with the sheen of his sweat. She trailed her fingers down his chest.

Gently, she eased off of him and lay at his side. He slipped his arm over her, cuddling with her. Gwrlais always turned his back to her and fell to sleep once he was satisfied. Being loved by Uthyr was all she had expected it to be and more so.

"I am exhausted." Eigyr turned on her side as did he, so she faced him.

"The night is not yet through. I would have all of you this eve." He gazed into her eyes. "I will know you in every way I can, for I may not have another chance to make love to you."

"You fear you might die at the king's hand … soon?" Her stomach grew queasy as guilt overtook her. She knew this was not her husband. This was the man who wanted to kill him. Yet she wanted him. Needed him. She loved Uthyr like she had never loved Gwrlais..

"Do not fret over me. The king and I will have our day and the best man will win."

This battle they fought was over her. She hated that. Still, she knew she wasn't responsible. Both Uthyr and Gwrlais were wrong. *The king shouldn't have flirted with a married woman. And Gwrlais should never have stormed out of the king's court or disobeyed Uthyr's command. Men.* "You are ready to lie with me again?" Her blood boiled at the thought of having his cock pulsating inside her once more.

"I cannot get enough of you." He slid his hand to her rear and stroked the plump checks. "You have such a beautiful ass. I want to pleasure you there."

Her heart raced. Gwrlais had never spoken of any desire to enter her through that orifice. It thrilled her to know every part of her body excited him. Just as he wanted more of her, she wanted more of him. She rasped, "Yes."

She felt his warm hands on her as he spread her butt cheeks. "To ease my entry." He rubbed the head of his cock there, slick with the rose scented oil she kept on the chest by her bed. Her skin tingled from the lubrication of his warm bulging flesh as he stroked her tiny opening in slow, circular motions.

He eased the head of his erection barely inside the taut opening. She sucked in a breath as he slid further, partway within the forbidden entrance. His iron-hard flesh was a firebrand inside her. The tightness eased as her inner walls stretched around his cock. Eigyr let out a deep groan of pleasure-pain.

With slow strokes, he glided his cock in and out to the rhythm of his heavy, ragged breathing. Eigyr's insides coiled in tension, demanding release. She arched her hips. He pushed deeper into her with each thrust.

More virile and creative, as well as more concerned with her pleasure. This definitely wasn't her husband. Gwrlais had been away from her many times before and he'd never come back any different than when he'd left, until now. She knew this was Uthyr.

Maddening pleasure pulsated in every vein of her body. She whimpered and shuddered in a spasm of release. Gwrlais groaned as his body quivered against hers.

He eased out of her, wrapped his strong arms around her waist and pulled her onto her back. He stretched out at her side. She leaned against the heat of his body as her breathing and heart rate slowed.

Cuddling her in his arms, he held her tight. Soon he drifted into a deep slumber. Eigyr couldn't sleep. The pleasure of the night left her as her thoughts weighted her down. *What have I done? Is this wrong?* She kept asking herself that question because she didn't want it to be wrong even if it was. Nothing would have stopped her from lying with this man even though she knew he had to be Uthyr.

Her gaze slid over Gwrlais's face. Her husband's face. She shut her eyes and looked at Gwrlais again. Uthyr. She saw Uthyr there.

Not Gwrlais' curly gray hair, narrow face, patrician nose, and pointed chin. But the unblemished face of a Celtic king. And she knew it well, for that face had haunted her dreams since the king's feast at Easter. She had found excuses to lie in bed, feigned exhaustion, just so she could drift to sleep and see that face. She didn't want to gaze at anyone or anything except Uthyr.

Every inch of him was broad and muscled, hard and strong, in prime form. Uthyr was all that was superb in a man, a true warrior king.

She'd had the wildest, coupling she'd ever experienced with a man who looked like Gwrlais, but was Uthyr.

What would she tell the priest and should she tell the priest? *Father, I had impure thoughts of another man as I lay with my husband or as I lay with a man who appeared to be my husband.* She knew in her heart that she had betrayed Gwrlais.

She laid her head upon his chest. His skin felt like warm sunshine and the comforting sensation quieted her guilty thoughts and lulled her to sleep.

SIX

Uthyr awoke with the scent of Eigyr dancing in the air and the warmth of her soft skin pressing against his. Her hair was a mess of red tangled curls. He couldn't stop smiling as they dressed. He felt buoyant and euphoric here with Eigyr. He'd been with far too many women to count, but none as aroused or passionate as Eigyr. Being with her felt so right. Now he longed to make love to her as she looked into his eyes. His true, undisguised eyes. He needed to be with her as Uthyr, for her to know who he was. Would it be the same? Would she give herself freely to a man other than her husband?

With his arm wrapped around Eigyr's shoulders, they strolled into the hall. There they sat at the feasting board, side by side.

He grinned at his companions, disguised as Jordan and Bricel, as they joined them to break their fast.

"I trust you slept well in your chambers?" he asked them while he spread honey on a slice of warm bread on his plate.

Amusement flickered in Ulfin's eyes. "We came upon two comely serving maids who couldn't sleep well. We followed them to our chambers. They knew the way having been there before. We all had a pleasant night."

Uthyr chuckled merrily. Ulfin and Menw rocked with laughter as well.

Eigyr tipped her face toward him. "What is it?" Her smile brightened. "What's so funny?"

He leaned his head toward hers and returned her smile. "It's nothing." Holding it to her lips, he fed her a piece of honey-coated bread. She took the bread into her mouth and chewed with zeal. Her eyes smoldered with desire. He knew his did the same. When she finished chewing, he covered her lips with his. She tasted sweet and hot.

Loud voices and the pounding of running feet alerted Uthyr. He broke the kiss and jerked his head toward the entrance of the feasting hall. Two messengers, still dusty from the ride, ran in.

One yelled, "Lady Eigyr, we bring the saddest of news. The duke has fallen."

The other one added, "Your dear husband Gwrlais is dead."

The breath caught in Uthyr's throat. *I have been found out.* Sadness beyond tears, equal in measure to the elation he'd felt but moments before, weighed him down, now. His one night with Eigyr had come to an end. *I must get away.* He gazed at Eigyr. She looked so vulnerable, head tilted to the side, eyes wide with shock. *I cannot leave her like this. I have to convince her the messengers are confused.*

He let out a soft chuckle and slid his arm over her shoulders. "Dearest wife, your own eyes do not deceive you, I am alive." He flashed a wide grin at her.

Both messengers took sharp gasps of breath, then gazed hard at him, seeming to study every line etched in his face. Suddenly, they stiffened.

The thin messenger said, "My lord, Duke Gwrlais, forgive me, but we just rode in from the siege."

The redheaded one broke in. "We traveled all night to bring the news to your lady wife. We saw your fallen body with our own eyes."

"So we thought," the other retorted. "When we rode out, everyone believed you were dead."

Ulfin, in the guise of Jordan, flashed a friendly smile. "But you see the duke is here with us."

"But do tell of the siege," Menw urged, appearing to all the world as Gwrlais' good friend, Bricel.

"Yes, well, the duke rode out shortly before twilight, when the king's army began to ram the walls." The redheaded messenger moved his hands excitedly as he spoke. "Gwrlais thought we could take them, but Uthyr's army was large and out-manned ours."

The slender messenger stepped forward. "So the duke fell, or so we thought, in the first thrust of battle."

The other one added, "And the town was taken as well."

With his arm wrapped around her, Uthyr gazed at Eigyr. "My love, as you can see, I did not fall in battle. They confused me with someone else. Yet, my heart breaks to hear Dimilioc is lost and so many good men killed. The king may come upon us here and take Tintagel. I will not let that happen. I must meet with him and make peace and put a halt to this madness and destruction."

Ulfin rose to his feet. "You are right, my lord, we need ride."

"I shall ride with you as well, Duke Gwrlais." Menw stood.

Uthyr gently pulled back from Eigyr, but the blue fire of her eyes captured and held his gaze. Unable to fight his aching need for a thirst only she could quench, he stood and pulled her to her feet. He crushed her to him. His mouth smothered hers in a demanding kiss. He twisted his lips over hers, so smooth and warm. With that memorable farewell kiss, Uthyr tenderly pulled out of her embrace. More than heat, moisture, and the taste of her lingered in that kiss. It sealed a silent, steadfast vow that he would make her his. She was the only woman for him. "Until I return."

She breathed lightly between parted lips, "Keep safe, Uthyr."

The two messengers glared at him with suspicion, but they were no match for the magic that had transpired this night. No one would get in his way, least of all two messengers form Gwrlais's war band.

Strains of scarlet appeared on Eigyr's face and her body stiffened. "Do not misunderstand. I had not finished my sentence, I was but asking of Uthyr."

She knew. Somehow she'd come to realize that it was he and not her husband who had lain with her.

She wheeled around to the two messengers. "You spoke of my lord, Gwrlais, falling in battle, but we know he is safe. Yet, you spoke not of Uthyr. I but ask, as what happens to the king is a matter of great importance for Britannia. If he dies, many nobles will vie for his crown." She shrugged. "Upon Uthyr's death, my Gwrlais would be free to make a claim for the kingship." She then turned to the man who looked like her husband. "Gwrlais, do you not want to know what happened to the king?"

He didn't know what to say. Had he imagined that she had called out his name? He must have, for now she spoke of Gwrlais usurping his throne. She didn't realize her husband was dead.

One of the messengers spoke up. "We heard nothing of Uthyr. All assume he is unharmed."

"I thank you for those tidings. Now, I must be off." Uthyr was overjoyed with news of Gwrlais's death. Also, he was grateful he hadn't had to deliver the fatal blow, as that would have only drawn Eigyr further from him. His only regret at the duke's death was the pain Eigyr would have at the loss of her husband. But now he had to leave. The longer he was here with these messengers, the more likely they would figure out that he was, in truth, King Uthyr.

Bricel gathered up their chain mail shirts and weapons. They helped each other into them and belted their swords at their sides. Uthyr dashed out of the hall and ran outside as Ulfin and Menw followed. Quickly, they mounted their horses.

"Fortune was with us that neither the true Bricel nor the real Jordan came to deliver that message," Ulfin quipped.

"It is so." Menw remained serene in tone and posture, as if he had known all along they wouldn't be caught.

Uthyr rode his horse at a trot, and as dawn broke over the mountain, he led Ulfin and Menw down the treacherous, narrow path. His cloak billowed in the wind. The salty tang of the churning sea below filled the air. The taste of the sea spray on his tongue reminded him of the taste of Eigyr's intoxicating flesh.

Knowing he'd soon return to his true appearance, Uthyr made his way free of the mountain path. As he rode in a dirt-kicking gallop across the wide open field toward the road to Dimilioc, he wondered if Eigyr would welcome him then.

Menw's mount galloped hard behind Uthyr's horse. The druid called out to his king, "Afore you ride up to your army looking like your dead foe, you should transform back to yourself."

Uthyr let out a hardy laugh, freeing all the pent up fear and excitement of the quest. "As you say, Menw."

As Uthyr reined in his horse, Menw and Ulfin did the same. After they dismounted, Uthyr took a deep breath, preparing for the change. He looked Menw in the eyes. The druid placed his hands upon the king's face and uttered the words,

"For truth's sake,
I bid unmake
the transformation,
reverse the application.
From Eigyr's husband
to king of the land,
from Jordan to Ulfin,
from Bricel to Menw,
restore us three.
So mote it be."

At Menw's words, a tinge of pain shot through Uthyr. His skin and muscles stretched in some places and shrank in others as he changed back to his own form.

He turned to the two companions at his side, and now saw the druid and his best friend as their true selves. "It's good to have you both back."

"You as well." Ulfin's wiry body, pleasing face, and animated smile had returned. "I was going mad, having to look at that ugly face of Gwrlais's. Chiefly, since I know he is now dead. It made me wary."

"Let it be," the druid said with a composed tone and gaze. "No one will ever know of what took place but the three of us."

Uthyr turned to Menw. "Druid, you have yet to name your price for the magic you wrought last night."

Menw gazed into the king's eyes. "With Eigyr free to remarry, you shall come to live with her in wedded bliss."

"In truth, but what is it you ask of me?"

"I told you of the child." Menw's voice was soft but firm.

"The great king of whom the comet foretold." Uthyr nodded.

"He will grow to be a victor and protector of the Celts." Menw's demeanor was calm, but as his eyes bore into Uthyr's it was clear, whatever he would ask, he would not take no for an answer.

Uthyr lifted his chin. "What is your price?"

"The boon I ask is to foster the child. Place him into my care. I shall raise him. For the task he is to complete, he needs the protection of the old gods, the blessing of the land in the ancient way."

"Would you take him away?" Uthyr stroked his chin. "I do not think his mother will stand for it."

"No, he will dwell with me in a sacred cave beneath Tintagel. She may visit him whenever she likes, and you as well. I will make it into a small learning center for my one and only pupil."

"I cannot say no, can I?"

"What must be, will be."

Powerful emotions reeled in him. The child was not yet born, but the pain of separation from the babe overtook him. He always imagined he would raise his son himself, yet he had given his vow and Menw had done his part as no other could. After all, fostering was a tradition. He'd been fostered by the archbishop Guethelin as a child. At least he and Eigyr would be close to the boy and see him daily. His voice broke as he pushed the words out of his mouth.

"At the age of six, I will hand my son over to you for

fostering. Make him the greatest king this land has ever known."

Menw nodded. "I shall raise him in our ways, befitting a true champion of the Celts."

"No other is as worthy as you to guide a young dragon on the path to being a king and a hero." He knew it was true. The child should be fostered by Menw. A wise man could raise a young prince to be just as wise. The girl, to come later, would be raised by him and Eigyr. He swallowed hard. Eigyr would be his wife. She would bear him children. His own family, his children to come, who would leave their mark on history long after he was gone — it was real.

He vaulted onto his horse as Bricel and Menw mounted theirs. Uthyr gazed at the rosy, golden haze of the dawn sky, remarkably free of clouds. The start of a new day. King Uthyr, with masterful balance, eased his stallion into a fast, free gallop to the road ahead.

Dear Reader,

Thank you so much for reading **Pendragon's Obsession**. I appreciate it so much. It's readers like you that make writing worthwhile.

I love Celtic history, myth, and legend. And this story from Geoffrey of Monmouth's' history of Britain is my favorite of the Arthurian tales. I always thought of it as the most sensuous story I've ever heard and because of that I wrote it as an erotica romance.

I tried to stay true to Geoffrey's telling of this legend as well as the history and belief system of the ancient Britons while also writing with the modern woman in mind. It was fun writing **Pendragon's Obsession** and I hope you had fun reading it.

I have two Arthurian novels, based on versions of stories from Geoffrey of Monmouth's' History of Britain: **The Celtic Fox** and **The Celtic Vixen.** They come as stand alones or together as a duology bundle in **Swords and Roses**.

With so many books out there, you do not know how happy you have made me by reading mine. I hope **Pendragon's Obsession** swept you away from the pressures and worries of the real world and brought a little magic to your life.

Thank you,

Cornelia Amiri

PLEASE SHARE YOUR ENJOYMENT!

If you would like to share your enjoyment of **Pendragon's Obsession** with others – please leave an honest review at any social media or bookseller websites.

For a free e-book of **The Scottish Selkie** and to keep up with my books and events, please subscribe to my newsletter at https://dl.bookfunnel.com/h2jrqxyfyo

Get your eBook autographed here. https://www.authorgraph.com/authors/CorneliaAmiri

Please visit my my twitter https://twitter.com/Corneliaamiri
    and my TikTok https://www.tiktok.com/@corneliaamiri2?lang=en

I can be contacted via Email and always appreciate feedback or comments about my books.

The latest information about my books and more can be found on my web site:
    http://CorneliaAmiri.com

ACKNOWLEDGMENTS

I also want to acknowledge my wonderful editor, Michelle Levigne. I appreciate her hard work and talent so much.

I also want to think Julie Darcy for her cover art for Pendragon's Obsession, which blew me away. I wanted to think Kyra Starr who did such a fabulous job of converting the cover for the print book.

I also wanted to think my wonderful critique partners, the talented multi-published authors, Lisa Carlisle and P. J. MacLayne. Their advice was immeasurable and greatly contributed to the completion and success of this book.

This book wouldn't be the same without Michelle, Julie, Kyra, Lisa, and Patricia. They have my deepest gratitude.

The Lynx and the Druidess

To Love A London Ghost

The Ghost Lights of Marfa

Starry Conquest

As Timeless As Magic

As Timeless As Stone

The Brass Octopus

I Love You More

Forged of Irish Bronze and Iron

Reach

A Boomer Chick's Bingo Card

Love AI Style - Bundle

Swords and Roses - Bundle

Warrior Hearts – Bundle

Need Fire - box set

Dancing Vampires - Box Set

Druidry and the Beast – full series

ABOUT THE AUTHOR

The Celtic Warrior Queen made me start writing professionally. I love history and in reading a book about the dark ages, I came across the rebel queen. She inspired me so much. I started jotting down notes, but they were fiction, visions of me involved in the Boudica revolt. Before I knew it, I had accidentally written a rough draft for a novel. And I've been writing books on purpose ever since. Drawing on my love of a happy ending, I have currently penned 35 published romance books.

I live amid the hustle and bustle of humid Houston, Texas with my muse, Severus the Cat. When not writing, I love to read, watch movies, and attend comic cons. I am working on a sequel to **Rare Finds**, and a sequel to **The Brass Octopus**, which I am also renaming and republishing as **The Librarian and the Rake**.